# HILARY McKAY

# PUDDING BAG SCHOOL

## A Strong Smell of Magic

Hodder
Children's
Books

A division of Hachette Children's Books

To Jim, who thought of the story

## CHAPTER ONE
### Class 4b, Pudding Bag School

Class 4b, Pudding Bag School, were taught to recognise the smell of magic by their teacher, Miss Gilhoolie. She thought it was very important.

A lot of people did not know what to think of Miss Gilhoolie. She seemed too cheerful for a teacher, and too pretty. She was very fond of diamonds (the bigger the better) and she wore them every day by the dozen. Her shiny bright green Ferrari also surprised people, and so did the way she could whistle through her fingers, and so did her short, tight skirts.

Class 4b thought she was a very good teacher.

"She may be bossy," said Dougal McDougal. "But at least she is not boring!"

Dougal McDougal was ten years old. He had red hair and lots of ideas, not all of them very good. His best friend was Simon Percy. Simon also had ideas, less than Dougal, but usually better. Simon was much quieter than Dougal, but then so was everyone else in Class 4b.

There were two classes of ten year olds in Pudding Bag School: 4a and 4b.

"Class 4a is the brainy ones' class!" said Class 4a. "Class 4b are all nutters! And Miss Gilhoolie is the nuttiest of all!"

"You're just jealous," said Dougal McDougal.

Miss Gilhoolie had a way of making lessons interesting. Science included popcorn making and panning for gold. The Geography Project survey was done by hot-air balloon. Class 4b's lessons were so unusual that none of them were surprised when they heard that 4b would not be joining any of the other classes on the school summer trip.

All the other classes were going to visit zoos and adventure playgrounds and open-air theatres.

"Very nice indeed," said Miss Gilhoolie to Class 4b. "We would do the same if only we could spare the time. Our class trip will be Purely Educational. Pass round these letters to parents, please Madeline, and make sure you all bring them back signed in the morning."

Class 4b grabbed the letters as Madeline handed them out and read them eagerly. Then they looked at each other in dismay. It seemed like the Class 4b school summer trip was going to be far from exciting.

This is what the letters said:

*Dear Parent/Guardian,*

*We hope your son/daughter will be able to join us on our annual summer trip. To keep costs to a minimum each student will need to bring a packed lunch, water bottle, and snacks for the journey. A small donation towards the cost of travel (not more than £3.00) would be appreciated but is not essential.*

*NB School uniform MUST be worn and (as usual) PLEASE no fizzy drinks!*

*Guinevere Gilhoolie*

*Please return the attached slip:*

-------------------------------------------------------------

*I give consent for ------------- (name of student) to take part in the summer class trip (A Practical Demonstration of the Smell of Magic)*

*I do/do not enclose a donation towards the cost of travel (please state amount)---------*

*Signed:------------------(Parent/Guardian)*

"But does magic smell?" asked Simon Percy (who was rather sorry to be missing the adventure playgrounds).

"Of course it does," said Miss Gilhoolie. "Everyone has smelt it, sometime or another. The trouble is that most people do not recognise it, which is a waste because it is there for a reason."

"What reason?" asked Madeline Brown (who would have loved to visit an open-air theatre).

"To warn you not to meddle," said Miss Gilhoolie, "and also (of course) to remind you to enjoy yourself. It is very important that you learn to recognise it and that is why we are going on this class trip."

"But how are we going to find magic to smell?" asked Samantha Freebody (who would have liked very much to go to the zoo). "What if we can't? It will be a complete waste of time!"

"Unless Miss Gilhoolie can do magic herself," suggested Dougal, cheerfully. "Can you do magic, Miss Gilhoolie?"

"Really Dougal, do I look like a witch?" demanded Miss Gilhoolie, and then just as Dougal was about to reply "Yes, very much," went on, "Of course, I can't conjure up the exact smell of real magic, but what I have arranged for you is a very good second best. It is often used for training purposes. Copy down this recipe in the backs of your Science and Technology books."

The recipe was:

*One large bottle of the most expensive French perfume*
*One large healthy hedgehog*
*One large barrow-load of freshly fallen snow*
*(preferably taken from a pine forest)*
*One boot cupboard full of well-worn old boots*
*A fresh west wind off the sea*

"Those are the standard ingredients," said

Miss Gilhoolie, briskly. "And anything else is fiddle-faddle! Yes, Simon dear?"

"Does it hurt the hedgehog?"

"Of course it does not hurt the hedgehog!" said Miss Gilhoolie. "You merely add the hedgehog to the boots, wait two minutes to allow the smell to infuse, pile in the snow (it will not bother the hedgehog at all as long as we brush it off again before it melts), pour on the perfume, and open all the windows so that the wind blows through. And there you are!"

"I should think," remarked Madeline Brown, who was very clever, "that you must have to be very quick. Otherwise, won't the snow melt and the hedgehog run away and the boots and the perfume get too strong to bear?"

"Timing is absolutely critical," agreed Miss Gilhoolie. "Now, it is a long way from here to a suitable coast with a reliable west wind from the sea, so I am afraid the coach will not be

able to wait for anyone who is late. I have hired an understanding fisherman's cottage, and the snow is being flown in from Norway by a friend of mine and will reach us at twelve o'clock. We will leave school at eight in the morning and there should just be time for one good sniff each before we have to come back. Any more questions?"

"It seems an awful lot of trouble," said Samantha Freebody.

"It will be worth it," said Miss Gilhoolie.

Just after twelve o'clock the next day Class 4b, rather stiff after their three and a half hour coach ride, filed one by one into the understanding fisherman's cottage, stuck their heads into the boot cupboard where the ingredients had been mixed, breathed deeply, said "Oh Miss Gilhoolie!" breathed again, and then filed out and back on to the coach for the long journey back home.

And all of them agreed that it had been worth it.

"I've smelt that smell before," said Madeline in class the following morning. "Not strong like it was yesterday, but lots and lots of times."

"I'm sure you have," agreed Miss Gilhoolie. "It is not at all uncommon. Very often when people smell it they say things like, 'You really should feel the air tonight,' or 'What's somebody cooking?' or, 'How that takes me back!' They know there is something special about, although hardly anyone can give it a name."

"Magic," said Madeline Brown.

For a day or two after that, people were very interested in tracking down things that smelt of magic. They went around sniffing and comparing notes.

"Books," said Samuel Moon. "It comes out of

books. Especially very old and very new ones."

"Rain on the pavements when the weather's been dry," said Charlotte.

"The dressing-up box," said someone else.

"Stones."

"Tents."

"The school basement smells of it sometimes," said Dougal. "And I smelt it once quite strongly coming out of the sweetshop. It was the first term Miss Gilhoolie was here. The day after that rocket we built went up."

"It didn't go up!" said Madeline. "Not just like that! You fired it!"

"I've said sorry," said Dougal. "I've said sorry loads of times, Madeline Brown! I didn't know you were in it!"

"Miss Gilhoolie smells of magic sometimes," remarked Simon dreamily, ignoring them both.

"She doesn't today though," said Emma, Charlotte's twin. "She smells of cough sweets.

**17**

Cough sweets, sore-throat sweets, and menthol inhaler."

"I noticed that hedgehog was sneezing!" exclaimed Dougal. "Miss Gilhoolie needn't bother getting ill now! It's the Summer Fair next week and our class still hasn't thought of anything to do. 4a are having a Bouncy Castle! I bet they win the Special Class Prize!"

The Special Class Prize was to be awarded to the class that made the most money at the Summer Fair. Nobody but the governors knew what it was, and that made it even more desirable.

Class 4a were behaving as if they'd won it already. They laughed at Class 4b, and said, "Poor old Nutters! You pathetic Moose Huggers just can't compete with the Brainy Ones' class!"

"Moose Huggers!" repeated Dougal, so indignantly that Class 4a howled with laughter.

"You do hug mooses!" they said.

"We are kind," said Dougal, "to one moose. Sir Lancelot. That is not moose hugging!"

Sir Lancelot was Class 4b's adopted lucky mascot. He was a scruffy moose belonging to Miss Gilhoolie. He spent his time tethered at the furthest corners of the playing field, keeping down the grass. He was a very plain animal and never smelt remotely magical, but even so Class 4b loved him. Madeline looked

across to where he stood, drooling moose-nut juice down his bony chest. How lucky they were, she thought, to have the sort of teacher who would keep a moose for a pet.

"Miss Gilhoolie is bound to think of something much better than a bouncy castle!" she said, but for once Madeline was wrong. Miss Gilhoolie refused to think of anything. She held her head in her hands and groaned at Dougal McDougal's explanations of the need for something exciting for the school summer fair.

"I dow know wob on earf your talbing abow!" she said. "Wob on earf is a Subber Fair?"

Many people began to explain what on earth a summer fair was, but Miss Gilhoolie exclaimed, "Dow'n tell me, dow'n tell me!" and flapped them away and sneezed.

Emma was right, she did not smell the least

bit magicky. She did not sound it either.

"Messing about with snow and sneezing hedgehogs just when the school fair is coming up!" said Dougal, very crossly as he walked home with Madeline and Simon that night. "She's caught an awful cold! It's as plain as plain!"

"Perhaps she'll be better in the morning," said Madeline, but Miss Gilhoolie was worse in the morning. She did not come to school at all. Instead she sent in messages for Class 4b, a list of work as long as a banner and instructions on the care of the moose.

"Don't let him get lonely," Miss Gilhoolie ordered.

Sir Lancelot did not get lonely. He became a sort of meeting point, or grumbling point, as Simon Percy remarked.

"I've just heard that 4a are having a candy-floss stall as well as a bouncy castle," reported

Samantha Freebody at lunchtime. "One of their dads is sorting it out."

There was deep groaning among Class 4b.

"They said 'Poor old Moose Huggers' when they noticed me listening," continued Samantha. "And they said why don't we have Pin The Tail On The Donkey and use Sir Lancelot for the donkey."

"They think they're so funny!" said Dougal bitterly. "Mind what you're doing with that bucket, Madeline! That was nearly my eye!"

"Sorry," said Madeline, mixing rolled oats and moose nuts (as instructed by Miss Gilhoolie) while Sir Lancelot fidgeted with impatience. "Do you think moose nuts smell a bit magicky?"

"Who cares if they do?" asked Dougal. "A bouncy castle and a candy-floss stall and we haven't got anything! Bother Miss Gilhoolie, messing about with snow and sneezing hedgehogs in all that wind! No wonder she's ill! She'd better be back tomorrow!"

But the next day Miss Gilhoolie was not back. Instead, she was in hospital, the terrible cold having turned into pneumonia. However, she did not forget Class 4b. From her hospital bed she sent more work lists, rolled oats and moose nuts, and enough homework to last for weeks.

That day Class 4a announced that two of their mothers had offered to organise a balloon race with real helium balloons.

"Balloons and a bouncy castle and a candy-floss stall!" moaned Dougal McDougal. "And we still haven't anything organised!"

Class 4b asked for help from the teachers who flew in and out of Miss Gilhoolie's class, delivering messages and setting work. They were no use at all. They suggested a book stall

23

(if enough books could be collected), a Guess The Weight Of The Cake competition (if a cake could be got hold of), a white elephant stall ("Where are we supposed to get a white elephant?" demanded Dougal), or helping the Infants with their Lucky Dip.

Class 4a laughed more than ever and suggested Spot The Flea on the Moose. They also told Class 4b that three of their dads had agreed to run a hot dog and hamburger stand.

"Why can't our parents do anything useful?" complained Dougal McDougal.

"They are all too busy," said Madeline.

That was true. Class 4b's parents were all things like ambulance drivers and firemen and mad professors, the sort of people who cannot take afternoons away to help at school summer fairs. Madeline explained this to Dougal as she flea-powdered Sir Lancelot after school.

"Well then, Miss Gilhoolie must be made

to help!" said Dougal, firmly. "I shall go and see her!"

"But she's in hospital," said Madeline.

"Then I shall go and see her in hospital," said Dougal McDougal.

## CHAPTER TWO
### Dougal in Disguise

Samantha Freebody said that she was sure that Dougal would not be allowed to go and see Miss Gilhoolie in hospital. It was not often that people agreed with Samantha, but this time they did.

"It's not as if you were a friend or relation," pointed out Charlotte.

"It's not as if you were going to be kind," said Emma.

"It's not as if you were grown up," said Samuel Moon.

Dougal said of course he was a friend, Miss

26

Gilhoolie was very fond of him, and of course he was going to be kind. Think how upset she would be if Class 4a won the Special Class Prize.

"Anyway, you don't know which hospital she's in," said Samuel.

It was very easy to find out which hospital Miss Gilhoolie was in. Dougal simply asked Mrs Pooter, the school secretary. Mrs Pooter was much too kind, and much too busy to suspect that Dougal was up to no good. She assumed that he wanted to send Miss Gilhoolie a Get Well card and she said that was very thoughtful indeed.

"I am sure she will be delighted to hear from you, dear," she remarked, as she wrote down the address, and she thought what a nice boy he looked, with his chestnut hair and his freckles and his innocent, shining eyes.

"Thank you," said Dougal, smiling at her

like the most angelic child in the world. Then he went off to boast of his cunning to the rest of Class 4b, gathered as usual in a grumbling huddle around Sir Lancelot the moose.

"Guess what this is!" he said, waving the slip of paper under Samuel's nose. "Miss Gilhoolie's hospital's address! Mrs Pooter gave it to me."

"She must be bonkers!" said Samuel. "Anyway, they'll never let you in!"

"They'll never keep me out!" said Dougal. "What are you all eating?"

"Moose nuts," replied Simon Percy.

"What do they taste like?"

"Pencil sharpenings," said Simon. "Mixed with treacle. Are you really going to try and visit Miss Gilhoolie?"

" 'Course I am," replied Dougal. "Someone's got to help us with the School Summer Fair. I'll tell her what 4a are doing and ask her if she can think of something really good for us.

Give me a moose nut, someone!"

Samuel handed him the moose-nut bag to help himself and Simon volunteered to come with him to visit Miss Gilhoolie.

Dougal chewed and swallowed and choked and spluttered and had to be banged between his shoulders for quite a long time.

"Crikey, moose nuts are disgusting!" he said when he had recovered. "No wonder Sir Lancelot looks like he does!"

"You swallowed them too quickly," said Samuel Moon. "They're all right if you chew

them for ages and ages like chewing gum. Are you going to let Simon go with you then?"

"I don't know," said Dougal. "I've been thinking about what you said about not being grown up. You might be right. There's lots of places kids can't go on their own. So it might be better if Simon didn't come because I may have to go in disguise."

Class 4b fell about laughing and choked on their moose nuts.

"I think it's a very good idea," said Dougal with dignity. "Could you get me one of your Dad's white coats, Madeline, do you think?"

"I suppose so," agreed Madeline, whose father was a mad professor and owned many white coats. "But what are you going to be disguised as?"

"A doctor of course!"

"You're not tall enough!"

"A short doctor!" said Dougal. "There's loads

of short doctors! A very short doctor in a white coat and I thought I'd put red-paint blood on it to make it look more real."

"Oh, let me come as well!" begged Simon Percy. "I want to be a short doctor with red-paint blood! Madeline could get a white coat for me too, couldn't you, Madeline?"

"Two very short doctors would be much too many!" objected Dougal.

"You just said there were loads of them!" protested Simon.

"Yes, but I don't suppose they go around together! Everyone would notice two very short doctors going round together!"

Simon could see that this might be true. And also he knew what a waste of time it was trying to argue with Dougal McDougal. So instead he asked, "Can I come with you and wait outside then?"

"Yes, that would be really good," said

Dougal generously. "And you can help me get ready too, if you like."

"We could use my new face paints to paint your face a proper doctorish colour," suggested Simon. "Greyish, I should think."

"And greenish," said Madeline, thinking of her father's friends.

"The doctor who I saw about my chickenpox was greenish and purpleish, like Sir Lancelot's tongue," said Charlotte, "although he did have grey hands."

Simon said he had all those colours in his face paints.

"You're going to look awful," said Samantha Freebody.

"I'm going to look perfect," said Dougal.

The disguising was done in Simon's bedroom after school that afternoon. They collected the white coat from Madeline's house and rushed back to Simon's for the face painting.

The results were very good. Dougal's face was coloured a doctorish greenish purpleish grey and Simon added white streaks in his hair. Red face paint splashed on the wrists and front of the white coat looked impressively gory.

"I think perhaps I look more like a surgeon than an ordinary doctor," remarked Dougal, admiring himself in the mirror.

"Perhaps you do," agreed Simon, and made him a badge with his badge-making kit.

EMERGENCY HEART SURGEON read the badge.

"Now all you need are some doctorish things in your pockets," said Simon.

That was easy to organise. Simon and Dougal ransacked the kitchen and the bathroom and the tool shed in the garden. Soon the pockets of Dougal's white coat were

bulging with vegetable knives and potato peelers, pliers and chisels, nail scissors and sticking plasters. A handkerchief that had been used to mop up some spilt red face paint added a perfect finishing touch.

"You're going to look a bit weird to people in the street when you get outside," remarked Simon, gazing at Dougal thoughtfully when they had finished. "I hope nobody rings the police!"

"Can't you lend me a coat or something to cover everything up?" asked Dougal.

Simon did his best, and eventually Dougal set off wearing Simon's mum's raincoat and Simon's dad's hat with Simon's gran's enormous umbrella held over his head. He was so completely covered that nothing could be seen of the Emergency Heart Surgeon, but still he was an unusual sight.

"Are people noticing me?" he asked from

under the umbrella as he and Simon walked along.

"Yes."

"Many?"

"Loads. I suppose it's the umbrella. It's such a dry day."

"Oh well," said Dougal, "I expect it will be worth it."

All the same it was a relief to reach the huge glass entrance of the hospital. There Dougal handed the coat and hat and umbrella to Simon, smoothed his bloodstained disguise, and marched boldly through the doors.

Dougal had not been able to imagine exactly what it would be like inside the hospital. He had thought pessimistically that he might be chased straight back out again, and he had thought optimistically that he might be invited to operate.

It had never crossed his mind that no one

would notice him at all.

Yet that is what happened. Just inside the doors a group of visitors were hovering around a large map of the building. Without even glancing up they made room for him to look as well. Miss Gilhoolie's ward was easy to find on the plan. Dougal set off a minute later and as he made his way down the corridors a man in a similar white coat to his own nodded and raised a hand as if he had met Dougal a hundred times before.

Dougal nodded back, held open a door for a blue uniformed nurse, and gave a thumbs up to a porter pushing a trolley. He began to feel quite at home and medical.

It was all so easy that by the time he reached Miss Gilhoolie's ward he was bouncing with confidence. He marched through the double doors with a rattle of knives and scissors and then he stood in the middle of the room pushing up his too long, blood-splattered sleeves and looked thoughtfully around.

This time he was noticed. Two old ladies burst into loud wheezy laughter and a third leapt from her bed and ran shrieking down the corridor. A nurse hurried after her, and another seized Dougal. She dropped him a moment later, having been stabbed by the potato peeler. This gave Dougal the chance to announce,

"I've come to see Miss Gilhoolie!"

From behind a curtain in the corner of the room there came a very loud groan and then a hoarse croaky voice called,

"It's all right, nurse. He's perfectly harmless! It's only Dougal McDougal."

"Miss Gilhoolie!" cried Dougal, dashing to the curtains and pulling them aside, and there was Miss Gilhoolie. She was propped up by

pillows and surrounded by medicine bottles, tissue boxes and bunches of flowers. She seemed to be passing the time by polishing a tray full of loose diamonds. She looked very pale and very ill and very, very cross.

"Dougal McDougal," she said, weakly but furiously. "What do you think you are doing?"

Dougal noticed the furiousness, but he also noticed the weakness and so he was not alarmed. He plumped himself down on the end of the bed, sniffed happily at the smell of magic that was arising from the flowers and the diamonds, and began a long account of the problems of Class 4b, Pudding Bag School, what with the Summer Fair coming up, and their teacher in bed, and Class 4a so rude and gloating, and not a useful parent between them.

After a while Miss Gilhoolie closed her eyes. "Don't go to sleep!" said Dougal, and started his list of complaints all over again.

"Summer fair," Miss Gilhoolie heard, repeated over and over. "Special Class Prize ... bouncy castle ... candy-floss stall ..."

Miss Gilhoolie slid down her pillows so that she was lying flat and a cascade of diamonds tumbled to the floor.

"Something better than a candy-floss stall is what we need," continued Dougal as he grovelled under the bed collecting them up again. "Moose huggers, that's what they've started calling us! ... Summer fair and nothing for us to do ... Balloon racing and hot dogs ... something better than Class 4a ..."

Dougal was a genius when it came to pestering. He had seven older sisters at home on whom he had constantly practised. He could keep it up for hours.

"Only two days away ..." heard Miss Gilhoolie for about the fortieth time. "...

better than a bouncy castle … something exciting …"

"Dougal!" moaned Miss Gilhoolie. "Go away!"

"But you haven't thought of anything yet," said Dougal indignantly, and began again. "… Fair … castle … candy-floss stall …"

"Whoever heard such rubbish?" demanded Miss Gilhoolie at one point. "Schools don't have fairs! There is nothing in my teaching contract about organising fairs!"

"Every year!" Dougal told her patiently. "Every year we have a fair! Everyone does something, every class I mean. This year there's going to be a Special Class Prize for the people who make the most money. Class 4a are saying they've won it already. They're having a bouncy castle and a candy-floss stall and hot dogs and a balloon race …"

"Yes, yes, you said," moaned Miss Gilhoolie.

"Go home now Dougal!"

"I don't think I ought to go home until you think of something," said Dougal virtuously. "They would be so disappointed, Simon and Madeline and Samuel and all the rest. I told you Class 4a are having a bouncy castle, didn't I?"

"Dougal," interrupted Miss Gilhoolie faintly. "I'll think of something. I will. But please go home!"

"It will have to be good," said Dougal. "Because Class 4a have got a bouncy ..."

"It will be good," said Miss Gilhoolie, pulling herself up and opening her eyes and trying to look firm.

"What, better than a b—"

"Better than a bouncy castle, of course! And a candy-floss stall and a hot-dog stand and a balloon race! Better than anything you've ever seen!"

43

"What is it then?" asked Dougal.

"Really Dougal!" exclaimed Miss Gilhoolie, almost as if she were well again. "Go home at once! I have told you I will think of something!"

"I only wondered ..." began Dougal.

"I will have it sent to the school."

"It's just because Class 4a ..."

"I know, I know! Talk about something else, please Dougal!" She sounded quite pathetic and Dougal was touched.

"Sir Lancelot misses you, Madeline says."

"Does he?"

"We all do. You won't forget, will you? About the fair I mean?"

"No, no. I'll remember the fair."

"I'll go then, shall I?" asked Dougal.

"Yes, please," said Miss Gilhoolie.

Outside the hospital Simon Percy waited and

44

waited. It was terribly boring. Simon counted cars. He counted aeroplanes overhead. He played the name game, where you give instant imaginary names to every stranger that passes. He worked out how he would spend a million pounds if he had a million pounds. He wrote his name in a mosaic of car-park pebbles, trained an ant to fetch grass seeds and worked out all the different days of the week his birthday would fall on until he was a hundred and two. After that he simply sat and stared at the hospital doors, and at last Dougal came out.

Dougal was very pleased with himself. He might not have been noticed on his way in to visit Miss Gilhoolie, but he had certainly been noticed on his way out again. His disguise had been admired by the whole hospital. The patient he had startled into running down a corridor had told him that doctors had given up hope of her ever walking again. He had been thanked by her relations, photographed for the hospital newspaper, interviewed on hospital radio and feasted on hospital food.

"But what about Miss Gilhoolie?" asked Simon.

"She's thinking of something," said Dougal.

"She's thinking of something," Dougal told Class 4b. They were out in the playground before school the next morning and he was trying to answer a storm of questions. "Yes, she still smells of magic! Well, of course she was pleased to see me! Loads of flowers! I suppose she did look illish! No, she didn't look pretty at all, Samantha! How could she, in bed? I didn't forget to tell her about the bouncy castle! I didn't forget anything! It's being sent to the school!"

"What is?" asked several people, but instead

of answering, Dougal pointed.

"That, I suppose," he said.

Four huge lorries were crawling slowly up Pudding Bag Lane, three green and one black. They turned into Pudding Bag School, entirely filling the car park.

## CHAPTER THREE
### What Came Out of The Lorries

An excited murmur began as Class 4b stared at the four enormous lorries.

"The school dinner food comes this time of the morning," said Samantha, but she sounded very uncertain and somehow everyone knew that this was no ordinary school dinner delivery.

"I'm sure it's not school dinners!" said Madeline. "Oh, I wish we could stay out here and watch them unpack!"

But that was not possible. The bell went for the start of morning lessons and they had to go and line up, along with the rest of the school, outside the cloakroom doors. To their astonishment nobody else seemed at all interested in the new arrivals to the school car park.

"Stop chattering, Class 4b!" ordered Mrs Pooter as she shepherded them inside. "Dougal McDougal, get in line and stop waving your arms about!"

"But have you seen ..." began Dougal.

"Please hurry up, dear!" begged Mrs Pooter. "My hay fever is dreadful in the mornings and I am ridiculously busy, what with Miss Gilhoolie being ill, and the Summer Fair only twenty-four hours away. Not to mention the fact that the Head was never properly replaced after whatever-it-was happened two terms ago (I never did hear the truth!)."

"If you mean Mr Jones being blasted into space in a home-made rocket, it's perfectly true," said Dougal helpfully. "I know because I was there at the time. In fact, I lit the actual match that blasted him!"

"Yes, and I'm sure you did it very nicely," agreed Mrs Pooter, shooing him into his classroom and not listening to a word. "Now then, sit down everyone! Do you think you could manage to take the register, Madeline dear? Then you must all choose library books and read them quietly until someone comes to sort you out. I will try to pop in from time to time but I cannot be running backwards and forwards from the office all day with all I have to do!"

"But Miss Gilhoolie usually issues our library books," said Samantha.

"I cannot help that," said Mrs Pooter. "You must issue your own. Someone must come to me for the key, someone must stamp them and someone else must take the tickets ... Please stop making difficulties, children dear!"

"Has Miss Gilhoolie sent any messages today?" asked Samuel, seeing that she was already edging her way towards the classroom door. "Because she told Dougal she would think of something for us for the school summer fair and we've just seen …"

"I'm afraid no messages today, dear. Now I really must go! Dougal McDougal!"

Dougal, who had been hanging halfway out of a window, trying to see round corners, came back in at the sound of his name.

"Dougal, close that window at once, please!" ordered the secretary. "It is setting off my hay fever for one thing, and for another, if you tumble out of it that will mean More Work For Me! I should have to ring your family and cart you off to Casualty and fill in goodness knows how many accident forms and I simply haven't got the time!"

"I was only looking at those lorries," Dougal protested. "They are huge! Three green and one …"

But Mrs Pooter was determined not to waste time listening to descriptions of lorries, no matter how huge and green. She was already out of the door.

"… black," said Dougal. "Three green and one black."

Mrs Pooter had gone, scuttling away like a hurried hen. She didn't see, and no one saw, the little man that climbed down from the leading lorry and headed into Pudding Bag School.

He walked straight to Class 4b, exactly as if he knew the way, and an astonished silence filled the room.

The little man had dandelion yellow hair, a pencil behind one ear and a clipboard in one hand. He was dressed entirely in green. He was even smaller than Madeline (although considerably fatter) but it was not his appearance that silenced Class 4b.

It was his smell.

He smelt exactly like a fisherman's boot cupboard when mixed with French perfume, a healthy hedgehog, pine-scented snow and a fresh west wind from the sea.

"Delivery for Mr Dougal McDougal!" announced this astonishing little man. "Delivery for Mr Dougal McDougal from Miss Guinevere Gilhoolie on account of his terrible pestering at the hospital last night! That's what I was told to say! And I was told to get Miss Madeline Brown to sign for it, her having more in the way of common sense!"

"Me?" asked Madeline.

"That was Miss Gilhoolie's instructions! And by the way she said Best Love to the moose and she'll be back on Monday, first

thing in the morning, to hear All About It."

Anything else the little man had to say was lost in the roar of excitement that followed, during which Dougal was thumped joyfully on the back several times and Madeline was pushed forward to sign the paper held out to her.

She would have done this very quickly if the little man had not said reprovingly, "You must never sign anything you haven't read first, my dear! You read it, and then you'll know what you're getting!"

So obediently Madeline took the paper and began to read aloud:

"Delivery Note for Contents Described Overleaf

Notes:

1. Contents not Suitable for Operation By

Children Under 36 Months

2.Trouble-Free Running of Contents Fully
Guaranteed.

3.Contents not to be altered, adjusted, oiled
or otherwise tampered with in any way.
Otherwise Trouble-free Running Not
Guaranteed at all!!!

("That is what they call the Get Out Clause,
my dear," explained the little man to Madeline.
"And they could not have put it plainer so
mind you take note!")

4.Contents to be left clean and tidy and
ready for collection at 6.00pm on the day after
delivery. Under NO circumstances will
contents be left any longer than the allotted
time.

"Now if all that sounds fair enough to you,"

said the little man to Madeline, "you must sign your name where I've put that cross. And then all that is left for you to do is to tell me where you want it putting!"

"But what is it?" demanded twenty-eight voices all together.

"Contents Described Overleaf," pointed out the little man, so Madeline turned overleaf and read aloud:

"One Galloping Pony Carousel (Live Action)

One Helter-Skelter (Lighthouse Style) ..."

"It's a fair!" shouted Dougal McDougal. "It's a fair for the Fair!"

"One set of Dodgem Cars (Sound Effect Models)"

Madeline could hardly make herself heard over the racket.

"One Triple Terror Express."

"And I must say Miss Gilhoolie only mentioned the first three items to me when we spoke," added the little man. "Highly unsuitable that last one, if you ask me! Needs adjusting very careful if it's to run with no catastrophes and we won't have time to see to it. Better leave it packed up."

"Leave it packed up?" repeated Dougal, unable to believe his ears.

"You've got plenty to be going on with as it is."

"Yes, but ..."

"Dougal!" said Madeline. "We've loads! A carousel and a helter-skelter and dodgem cars! It doesn't matter about the ... about the ... What actually is it, anyway?"

"That's what I want to know, too," said Dougal, greedily.

"Well," said the little man, putting on a pair of round spectacles in order to look more closely at Dougal. "It's usually known in the trade for convenience sake as one of those

58

little trains. But the full name (the name that goes down in the accident books) is The Triple Terror Spine Freezing Icy World Express."

"Oh, lovely!" breathed Dougal.

"Lovely is what it is not," said the little man sternly. " 'orrible is what it is. And if it wasn't down on the delivery form I would think it had been sent by mistake."

"Miss Gilhoolie never makes mistakes," said Dougal.

"Then she must be One in a Million," replied the little man. "Anyway, you forget about it and concentrate on the roundabout and whatnot. That'll be enough for the likes of you. Now, as there is Nothing Like Now and Time is Time, perhaps one of you will tell me where you would like it all put."

"What about over by the moose?" suggested Madeline.

"Is it a reliable moose?" asked the little man, looking sharply at Madeline over the top of his spectacles.

"Oh yes," said Madeline. "Oh, I am sure he is! Very reliable indeed I expect!"

"Then," said the little man magnificently, "Over By The Moose It Is!"

And with that he was gone.

Class 4b's windows looked straight on to the corner of the playing field occupied by Sir Lancelot the moose. They spent the whole day watching, and gradually, behind the section roped off by the little man and three other little men exactly like him, a fair seemed to grow out of the grass. Mrs Pooter, who scuttled in to see them from time to time, refused to take any interest in the view at all. She cried, "Children dear, don't bother me!" and never once glanced at the little green and

yellow men, hurrying about like animated
dandelions between their lorries and the
moose. Even when other teachers asked what
on earth was going on she simply clasped her
head and moaned, "Don't mention Summer
Fairs to me!"

It was a very long day for Class 4b. They
hardly knew what to do to make it pass more
quickly. They hung out of the windows until

Mrs Pooter locked them shut, and they read their library books until not even Samuel, the class bookworm, could bear to turn another page, and they got hotter and hotter and more and more on each other's nerves.

"Think of something we can do," they begged Madeline, because she was the class brain and usually got the job of thinking what to do.

Finally she did.

"We could work out a rota for looking after the rides," she suggested. "To make sure that everyone has plenty of chances to have turns on everything."

Dougal said he did not want to be on a rota. He said he was only interested in the Triple Terror Express.

"We're not using that one," Samantha reminded him, primly. "The little man said."

"Yes but he's gone now, isn't he?" said

Dougal. "So what's to stop us?"

"Dougal McDougal!" exclaimed Samantha in a very shocked voice.

"What?"

"Fancy talking like that! After Miss Gilhoolie has gone and sent us this lovely fair and the little men have worked so hard putting it up. I think that is so awful ..."

"Samantha, don't!" begged Madeline

"... and wrong and greedy," continued Samantha, ignoring her. "And when the little men come back you'll get us all in trouble ..."

"I don't see what it's got to do with you," said Dougal rudely.

"Selfish!" said Samantha. "That's what it is!"

"Gosh!" said Dougal, now completely annoyed. "Whose fair is it anyway, Samantha Freebody? Mine! It was delivered to me, in case you didn't notice! But I will kindly share the dodgems and the helter-skelter and that roundabout thing with the rest of you because I am NOT selfish and I will kindly keep the Triple Terror Express for me because I WANT to and that is that, so there!"

"Tell him not to, Madeline!" said Samantha.

"I don't think I can," said Madeline. "I think it's too late. Dougal is very stubborn …"

"Yes I am," said Dougal.

"… and bossing him about is the worst way of getting him to do anything …"

"Yes it is," said Dougal.

"So we will have to put up with him having what he wants. Although it would be very nice if he would help with the other things too, if he doesn't mind."

"Of course I don't," said Dougal. He and Madeline had been great friends ever since she had forgiven him for accidentally blasting her into deepest space. If the conversation had ended there and Samantha had said no more,

Dougal might have allowed himself to change his mind about the Triple Terror Express, and everything would have been all right.

But Samantha said, "You always have to show off, Dougal McDougal! Anyway, I don't believe you'd really ever dare!"

Madeline groaned, and Simon groaned and several people said reproachfully, "Oh Samantha!" but it was too late. Now, whether he liked it or not, Dougal was stuck with the Triple Terror Express. No one had ever said Dougal wouldn't dare do something that he did not immediately go and do.

"You wait, Samantha Freebody," said Dougal McDougal. "You just wait! I'll show you what I dare!"

Right at the end of the afternoon something unexpected happened. Mrs Pooter came in and said since they had been so good, working alone with no trouble or squabbling (Dougal quickly clamped a hand over Simon's truthful mouth) they could go outside and have a look at Miss Gilhoolie's contribution to the school summer fair.

"And try it out?" asked twenty-eight voices.

"I suppose so," agreed Mrs Pooter. "Just for a few minutes. That is all the time I have to spare. I will bring out some work to do while you play."

If she had said that she would bring out some lions to tame while they played they would not have taken any notice. They streaked out of the classroom and down the stairs and through the school and across the playing field and then they pulled back the green canvas covers that the little men had left over their rides, and they stared and stared and stared.

Nothing they had seen or dreamed or

imagined or hoped for was as good as Miss Gilhoolie's contribution to the school summer fair.

The Galloping Pony Carousel was the first thing to be set in motion, dappled ponies of gold and silver with red and green saddles and bridles, each on a silver and gold twisted pole. In the centre was a barrel organ and two large buttons, green to go and red to stop.

Emma and Charlotte, who were twins and who dreamed constantly of ponies, discovered that afternoon what it is like to have dreams come true.

"They come alive!" shrieked Emma, who happened to be the first to mount a pony, and she was right. No sooner did the rider climb into the saddle than the golden ears began to flicker, silver manes tossed, and painted bodies grew warm and began to breathe. As the music

began the twisted poles seemed to melt
completely away and the ponies began a canter
that became a gallop. Faster and faster turned
the carousel, and like the wind went the ponies.

"They're racing!" squealed Charlotte,
clutching her pony's mane, and so they were,
racing so fast that the fairground blurred into
a rainbow of light, and there was nothing to
be seen except a circle of colour, and the
running ponies, and nothing to be heard
except the wild, jangling music of the barrel

organ, the light drumming of silver hoofs, and shrill neighs of delight.

When the carousel finally stopped it felt for a moment like the world had stopped with it. The riders slid down from their painted ponies and gazed at each other, dazzled and disbelieving, and all round them was the smell of magic.

The Lighthouse helter-skelter was a much quieter affair altogether. There was a pile of mats at the bottom and a staircase that spiralled round and round the inside of the red and white striped tower until it reached a circular balcony at the top. In the centre was a great revolving light enclosed in a diamond cut-glass ball so that a thousand glitters dazzled the eyes. There was a railed barrier enclosing the balcony and a little flat platform where you placed your mat before sitting down and whizzing round and round to the bottom of the tower. Simon Percy did not sit down straight away, but turned his back to the dazzling glitter and looked outwards over the railed barrier.

Far away, deep in the blue, he saw a sailing ship. He rubbed his eyes and looked again and dolphins were leaping. Beside him Samuel Moon said in a stunned whisper,

"Look at the waves!"

There was seascape after seascape, which changed as Simon moved around the balcony, desert islands and flying fish, pounding waves and rocky headlands. They lasted until he inadvertently stepped on to somebody's mat on the starting platform, and found himself shooting down the slide. He would have climbed straight back up for another go at once if Madeline had not grabbed him and shouted.

"Come and look at the dodgems!"

The dodgems were a whirl of colour. There were old-fashioned fire engines with large brass bells, ice-cream vans playing ice-cream music, traction engines that blew out steam with ear-splitting whistles, a double-decker bus that you drove from upstairs and a miniature Silver Ghost Rolls-Royce that purred like a cat. Also there was a bright red Ferrari, a yellow combine harvester, a safari Jeep and a long, low, pale pink saloon. They did not crash, but bounced from each other as if held apart by invisible force fields, and they went very fast. As they turned and cornered great spurts of coloured stars shot from their wheels.

Dougal McDougal was saving the best till last. He had ridden on a silver-dappled pony, slid twice down the helter-skelter, and done handbrake turns on a combine harvester in a cloud of green sparks. His expectations

could not possibly have been higher as he ran
to pull the covers off the Triple Terror Spine
Freezing Icy World Express.

## CHAPTER FOUR
### The Triple Terror Spine Freezing Icy World Express

The little train (as it was known in the trade) was the only ride still covered up.

"I'll uncover it myself," Dougal said when Simon and Samuel kindly offered to help. "I bagged it!"

The covers were much shabbier and dirtier than the ones that had been over the other rides. Dougal began pulling them away and the first thing to appear was a blackboard.

In twirly curly writing it gave a description of what was in store for anyone who was planning to take a ride. It read:

> *Pass Through the Icy Cavern!*
> *Vanish Utterly Into The Dark!*
> *Explore Dramatic Dragon Land and ...*
> *Appear For Your Free Colour Photograph*
> *Under The Blaze Of The Northern Lights!*

Oh, thought Dougal, and something deep inside him gave a very small twinge of disappointment, because it wasn't quite what he had expected of a Triple Terror Express. He felt slightly worried as he tugged away the rest of the covers.

Underneath was a round raised platform with steps up one side and the green grass of the playing field showing dimly underneath. The whole thing was obviously put together in sections like the slices of a cake. Around the platform ran a little circular metal track, two thirds of it hidden under a dirty, black canvas tunnel. On the part of the track that was out in the open there stood a little train, four small open carriages strung together behind a battered looking engine. Beside the entrance of the tunnel was a single green button labelled "GO".

That was all. There was not a trace of the smell of magic that lingered round the carousel, or was carried in the breeze that blew on the top of the lighthouse, or arose from the clouds of coloured stars that streamed behind the dodgems. The Triple Terror Express smelt of musty old canvas and rust and damp.

Dougal stared at all this, the little track and the train and the canvas tunnel, and he was completely baffled.

"The surprise must be inside," he said at last, and climbed aboard. Simon and Samuel,

Charlotte, Emma, Madeline and Samantha all climbed aboard too.

Then Dougal reached out and pressed the green button and the engine clanked to a start.

There were swing doors at each end of the tunnel. The entrance ones creaked open as the engine pushed into them, and then they were inside.

It was not hard to guess where they were. There was a cotton-wool snowman beside the track, plastic icicles dangling from the roof, and a large pole in the middle, like a single candle in the centre of a cake. This pole was painted in blue-and-white spiralling stripes and was labelled: NORTH POLE

"So this must be the Icy Cavern," remarked Simon, trying to sound very cheerful.

"Icy Cavern? It's not even chilly!" said Samantha scornfully. "I'm sorry to tell you Dougal, but your ride's absolutely rub ... Ow!

76

Why are you poking me, Madeline? Where are we going now?"

The little train was pushing through thick black curtains. They caught against Dougal's face, and tangled in the bobbles on Samantha's pony tail.

"I suppose this is us vanishing into the dark," said Samuel helpfully. "It is dark ... sort of ..."

"It said 'Utterly' though," objected Samantha. "Vanish Utterly Into The Dark, it said! I wouldn't call this Utterly! Why are we stopping? Is that cartoony-thing by the North Pole supposed to be a dragon?"

"Yes, I think it probably is," said Simon.

"Of course it is!" said Madeline loyally. "It's a very good dragon! Look, there's two more on the other side! I wish I could draw dragons like that!"

"Dramatic Dragon Land," said Charlotte, gazing around. "Well, I suppose they are

77

dramatic enough! Because how dramatic would you want a dragon to be? Really dramatic would be awful! It's nice that the train stops to let you look properly. It's very good, Dougal!"

"Yes, very good," murmured Dougal's friends in agreement, all except Samantha, who observed, "some people are afraid of telling the truth!"

It was while they were halted in Dramatic Dragon Land, gazing at the luminous paintings of cartoon dragons on the inside of the tunnel walls, that a string of pink and blue light bulbs strung across the roof suddenly switched on.

"Why?" asked Samantha, and for a minute no one could answer until Emma suddenly exclaimed.

"It's the Northern Lights, of course! Don't you remember, like it said on the board? Appear for your free photograph under the blaze of the Northern Lights! Soon it will be the photograph, I expect. Smile!"

"Smile!" said Samantha. "I'm not smiling! I think it's rubbish."

Just as she spoke there was a bright flash, a loud click, and the train started up and chugged back into daylight again. As it came to a halt a small sticky picture was delivered from a slot (like the slot in a photo booth) under the green button for GO.

"It's us!" said Samuel, trying to sound pleased. "Partly!"

Mostly, it was Samantha, with the top of her head cut off, just about to say "Rubbish!"

"It's not very good of me," said Samantha, critically. "And Dougal looks like he's about to burst into tears! I'm not surprised. That was the most useless rotten ride I've ever been on. There's nothing magic about it at all."

"I think it was very good indeed," announced Dougal.

His friends stared.

"It's nice and peaceful," said Dougal stubbornly. "It's like a real proper fair ride. Not miles high up and far away like that helter-skelter ..."

"But the helter-skelter is wonderful from miles high up," protested Simon.

"... or all out of control and bouncy, like those ponies ..."

"Oh, Dougal!" exclaimed Charlotte and Emma reproachfully.

"... and those dodgems ..."

Here Dougal paused. He had loved the dodgems most of all. It was almost impossible to think of one bad thing about them.

"They are probably very dangerous!" he said at last. "And definitely much too fast!"

"Well, nobody drove as fast as you!" said Samantha indignantly. "You whizzed, Dougal McDougal! We could hardly see you for smoke and sparks! I think …"

But what Samantha thought was never known because at that moment Samuel Moon had the good fortune to find a caterpillar on a daisy stalk. He picked it up and held it towards her.

"I hate caterpillars!" cried Samantha and ran away shrieking.

Everyone sighed with relief.

"Come on," said Simon, as Samuel gently replaced his caterpillar. "What'll we go on next?"

"Packing up time in five minutes!" called Mrs Pooter across the field.

"I'm having another ride on my lovely train," said Dougal. "A ride on my own!" he added, seeing his friends' horrified faces. "You can go off and do as you like."

Charlotte and Emma looked at each other, murmured, "The ponies …" and were gone.

Simon's eyes turned towards the lighthouse. Madeline and Samuel glanced guiltily at the dodgem cars. Nobody moved though, except Dougal, who climbed back on to his little train.

"I wish you'd stop staring," he complained as the engine began its rattling start. "Go away!"

His friends took one step backwards. Madeline raised her hand.

"Clear off and don't wave!" growled Dougal over his shoulder, and he was still growling as he disappeared into his dismal canvas tunnel.

"He wasn't crying," said Simon.

"Definitely not," agreed Samuel.

"Of course he wasn't," said Madeline crossly. "Come away quick! He won't want us looking at him when he comes out."

Dougal could not believe his bad luck. This

time the train seemed even slower, the icy cavern warmer, and the black curtains more tatty and worn. This time he hardly saw the dragons or the Northern Lights and he completely missed the North Pole. The photograph that appeared at the end of the journey was so shameful that he ripped it up with scarlet cheeks.

"Poor, poor Dougal," said Samantha Freebody, as they lined up to go back to the classroom, and Dougal overheard and that was the worst part of the afternoon of all.

None of Dougal's friends were unkind enough to walk home with him after school that day. He plodded home alone and was so grumpy with his family, and smelt so strongly of mildew, that even his favourite sister Kate complained. He refused to eat pasta or sausages or pizza or anything else his mother could think of. He told his father that football was boring and went early to bed.

Dougal's was not a very restful bedroom. The sheets were gritty with broken moose nuts fallen from his pockets, the mouldy remains of three or four packed lunches glowed strangely on the windowsill, Madeline's father's bloodstained coat made an unpleasant heap on the floor. All through the hot light summer evening Dougal tossed and twisted. He wished that he had never disguised himself and visited Miss Gilhoolie, or seen a lorry in the school car park, or listened to a little green and yellow man. He wished that Samantha Freebody went to a different school in a different town on another planet in an unparallel universe. But most of all he wished that he had never seen or heard of the totally rubbish, completely boring, absolute waste of space that was the Triple Terror Spine Chilling Icy World Express.

For the hundredth time Dougal went over the words of the little man who had delivered the fair.

"If it wasn't down on the delivery form I would think it had been sent by mistake,"

"Highly unsuitable ..."

"Needs adjusting very careful if it's to run with no catastrophes ..."

"... the full name (the name that goes down in the accident books) is The Triple Terror Spine Freezing Icy World Express."

"Lovely is what it is not!"

"He must be mad!" thought Dougal crossly, and fell asleep.

The next thing Dougal knew was that it was early morning. Very early morning.

Outside the light was only just silvery grey but the birds were singing as loud as road drills and the milkman was dropping his bottles in the street. Indoors, the cat was rattling at the cat flap and the cuckoo clock was calling four and Dougal's father and mother and seven elder sisters were fast asleep and snoring because they were used to the racket that was night-time in the McDougal house.

Only Dougal was awake.

Dougal was not the sort of person who wakes up in sleepy bits and pieces. He was ready for the day the moment he opened his eyes, and in the night his brain had solved the problem of the Triple Terror Express.

"It needs properly adjusting!" he announced, jumping out of bed and running down the stairs, pausing only to grab a bunch of carrots and a large can of spray-on bike oil from the kitchen. Seconds later he hurried out of the noisy, sleepy house.

He went to school in his pyjamas.

Sir Lancelot (that reliable moose) was very pleased to have an early morning visitor, especially one bringing carrots. He chewed them up greedily, dribbling carrot juice down his already moose-nutty front. When the carrots were all gone he chewed Dougal's pyjamas instead.

"Let me go, you daft moose!" said Dougal. "I've got stuff to do. There's one of the rides needs fixing … Oh all right, come with me if you want … Don't lick my neck! Come over this way!"

He led Sir Lancelot over to the little train and pulled away the stained canvas cover. Somehow, in the shining light of early dawn, it looked even shabbier, but Dougal, with the oil spray in his hand, was no longer downhearted.

"It definitely needs oiling," he told Sir Lancelot. "Look at all that rust on the wheels! And then it needs adjusting ... I wonder where you do that. I'll get it oiled first."

Dougal loved oiling things and Sir Lancelot seemed just as keen. Together they sprayed oil until it dripped from the wheels and the links between the little carriages.

"Still loads left!" said Dougal, shaking the can when the wheels and links were finished. "I'm going to do the whole track!"

Dougal began his oiling of the whole track by the simple method of starting the train and leaning over the front of the engine with the oil can, spraying as they went along. It worked very well until he accidentally dropped the can. The little train chugged over it, bursting it open, which meant that Dramatic Dragon Land was very well-oiled indeed.

"Flooded," said Dougal, leaning over and mopping a bit with his pyjama sleeve. "Never mind. It will stop it going rusty, anyway. Now for the adjustments."

Sir Lancelot (who was also rather well-oiled by this time) took great interest in the adjustments. He followed Dougal closely as he walked round and round the outside of the platform, inspecting the construction of the little train.

"So as I can take it apart," he explained to Sir Lancelot. Sir Lancelot looked thoughtful.

The six slices of the circle that made up the Triple Terror Express were fastened together with bolts. Two of the slices were the open track where the train stood when it was not in use. The other four were under the canvas tunnel. Each of them was labelled on the side in white paint: Icy Cavern, Vanish, Dragons, Northern Lights. Dougal could see nothing that would adjust.

"I'm looking for switches," he explained to Sir Lancelot. "Or controls or dials or levers or buttons. What's the matter?"

The moose was jabbing very eagerly at the side of the platform with his hoof.

"Oh, the bolts!" exclaimed Dougal. "Do you think I should unfasten them?"

Sir Lancelot wagged his head up and down and a moment later Dougal had the first of them undone, and soon after that a section of platform completely detached from its neighbours.

"I wonder if it pulls out," he said, and began tugging experimentally. It was immensely heavy (and Sir Lancelot did nothing at all to help) but eventually it came free and moved out from the circle a little, like a slice of cake half chosen on a plate.

That left a gap that could be peered into. Sir Lancelot twisted his head almost upside down and stared interestedly underneath.

"It's on wheels," Dougal told him, now on his hands and knees, "but there's a little space … It would be a bit of a squash but if I were to lie down on the grass I could pull myself right underneath …"

Sir Lancelot encouraged this idea by giving Dougal such a hard shove that he fell forward and banged his nose.

"You really are a very bossy moose," he complained, but all the same he turned on to his back and began to drag himself under the Triple Terror Express. "I don't suppose there's anything under here anyway … just Works … like under a car … Oh, I've found some writing! It looks like … Oh! Oh, fantastic! It's a control panel!"

"NO UNAUTHORISED ACCESS!" read the control panel in bright green glow-in-the-dark letters, and underneath:

"To Reset Controls Press *."

"Hurray!" shouted Dougal to Sir Lancelot, and unhesitatingly pressed *. At once there was a strong smell of magic which he completely ignored.

Once Dougal had found that first control panel it was not difficult to discover the rest.

"Icy Cavern", read the dial belonging to the next section, and Dougal, squeezed into the tiny gap between grass and controls, banging his nose, catching his hair, half blinded by oil drips and half suffocated by the smell of magic that was pouring all around him, turned it up from "Min" to "Max".

"Darkness Levels," said the writing by the switch on the next panel he found. Dougal turned it from "Min. (Simulated)" to "Max. (Utter and Complete)".

Dramatic Dragon Land had three settings: "Illustrated", "Animated", and "Live". Dougal turned it from "Illustrated" to "Live". After that he switched the Northern Lights from "Back Up" to "Main", and then he dragged himself out into the open air again and blinked with surprise.

It was bright morning. The grey light of dawn had passed completely. The sun was high in the sky, the dew had dried, and Pudding Bag Lane was humming with traffic.

"I must have been under there for hours," said Dougal in surprise to Sir Lancelot, as he toiled to push the section he had detached back into place. "Simon and Madeline and everyone will be here any minute! Gosh, it would have been awful if Madeline had caught me making adjustments … Can you imagine the fuss she would have made!"

Sir Lancelot looked very uncomfortable at these words. He would not look at Dougal, and he turned his back on the newly adjusted Triple Terror Express. He concentrated on biting the grass. His face took on the expression of a good reliable moose, innocently eating breakfast.

"Anyway, it's done now, and it's probably wonderful, and I didn't get caught," said Dougal. "I must just have one go … Ow! Yuk! Put me down, you're dribbling all down my legs! What's the matter with you?"

For Sir Lancelot had suddenly abandoned his breakfast and grabbed Dougal by the back of his pyjama trousers. Dougal twisted and wriggled and implored him to let go but it was no use. Sir Lancelot held him firmly and he could not escape. It was not until people actually began to come into sight, through the playground gates and on to the grass of the playing field, that he released Dougal. Then there was no time to do anything, except tug the covers back over the ride, and run for home as quickly as possible before anyone spotted him.

"So long as I don't meet someone I know!" he told himself as he ran, because the thought of meeting someone he knew in the state he was in (barefoot, grass stained, oil covered, scratched, filthy and in moose-chewed pyjamas) was much worse than the thought of meeting someone he didn't. Someone he knew would demand explanations.

Dougal was lucky. He passed plenty of people, but none of them recognised him. He made it all the way home without having to say more than "Sorry" and "Excuse me" and "I didn't mean to do that. I hope it didn't hurt". His plan was to dress, rush back to school, move the unhelpful Sir Lancelot as far away as possible from the little train, and try out his ride at last.

But unfortunately, the moment he dashed into the house he met his mother.

Who happened to know him very well indeed.

## CHAPTER FIVE
### The Summer Fair

Dougal's mother took control of his morning. He was scrubbed, scolded, fed, hugged, carted off to the doctor to have his bruises and scratches and moose bites inspected, injected in case he got tetanus, de-oiled, grounded for a week and sent to his room. He was just climbing out of his window when his lovely big sister Kate came in.

"I've got your grounding reduced from a week to a day," she said. "And starting tomorrow instead of now. So come on! You're allowed out to the school summer fair if I

97

come with you to make sure you are good ..."

Kate really was, thought Dougal, as he had thought many times before, the best sister in the world.

All the same he had missed hours and hours of the fair. When he arrived the school field was seething. The bouncy castle was uproarious with toddlers and the carousel was spinning like a captured planet. The air was filled with floating balloons, and the equally delicious smells of fresh candy floss, hot dogs, fried onions and magic. Everywhere there was music and shrieks and the swoosh of people whizzing down the helter-skelter.

One of the people who swooshed down was Simon.

"Dougal! Dougal!" he shouted, grabbing him. "Where have you been? Come with me! You come too, Kate! There's icebergs now and we've just spotted a whale!"

A whale was impossible to resist. Simon was
already racing back up the spiral staircase of
the helter-skelter and Dougal tore after him.
At the top he found a group of his friends all
exclaiming and pointing with delight. A new
view had just appeared: killer whales leaping
among the ice floes of a distant arctic sea.

"If you listen really hard you can hear the
splashes," said Simon to Dougal, "and the
cracking creaking sounds must be the ice!
Those whales are in a real sea! But you can
only see it if you look outwards. If you look
downwards it's just grass."

Dougal looked downwards and saw the
Triple Terror Express alone and forlorn in a
corner of the field.

"There didn't seem much point in
uncovering it," said Simon, following his gaze.

"Not much point?" repeated Dougal. "You

wait and see!" And he slid down the helter-skelter, hurried across the field, dragged away the covers and looked affectionately at his shabby little train.

"I bet you are the best thing here!" he said.

He was about to climb aboard and check this out for himself when two things happened.

The first was the sudden appearance of three boys from what Dougal and his friends called Big School.

The second was the arrival of Sir Lancelot the moose, who charged across the field at a gallop and tripped up Dougal so that he fell flat on his face.

"Quick! Before the kid gets up!" said the biggest of the big boys, and he vaulted into the first carriage and pressed the GO button while his friends jumped in behind.

"Oy!" yelled Dougal. "It's 50p each! You

haven't paid me yet!"

They jeered and disappeared into the tunnel. Sir Lancelot hauled Dougal upright with his teeth.

"I'll get them when they come out!" growled Dougal furiously, and went and positioned himself at the exit end of the tunnel, ready to pounce.

He waited and waited.

For a very long time.

During which nothing happened.

And then finally there came the sound of clanking and the little train reappeared, but there were no big boys inside. Clearly they had sneaked out before the end of the ride, pushed under the canvas and escaped.

"What a cheat!" yelled Dougal, dancing with rage, rushing round to peer under the canvas, rushing back to peer into the train and then tearing off into the crowds in the centre of the playing field, determined to find his burglarous customers. "What a swiz! Where are they? Oh, get out of my way, Sir Lancelot!"

From the centre of the crowd he had caught a glimpse of the little train, and another customer, Mrs Pooter, reading the notice. But the crowds were very thick. By the time he and Sir Lancelot had fought their way back out again, she had gone.

"Changed her mind," Dougal told Sir Lancelot. "Oh, please stop doing that! Mooses don't buck! It just looks silly. Anyway, you'll kick someone. I'm tying you to the fence."

Sir Lancelot disliked this idea so much he lay down in protest. It was only with great difficulty that Dougal was able to get him tethered.

"Good!" he exclaimed, when he had finally managed. "Now I can try out my ride at last! Oh no!"

Two exhausted-looking mothers were approaching, each pushing empty double buggies. Behind them followed four grizzling toddlers.

"Want to go wound and wound!" they wailed as their mothers began packing them into the carriages.

"It's fifty pence each," announced Dougal, panting up to them.

"Fifty pence!" exclaimed the mothers. "Each? We just wanted somewhere to leave them for a few minutes. Anyway, don't Under Threes Go Free?"

"No!" said Dougal, outraged. "Definitely not! In fact they should cost twice as much because they're so sticky. That one with the ice cream's dripping all over the seats! I think you should take it out."

"Well!" said the toddlers' mothers. "That's not a very nice way to talk! Are you going round with them?"

"No I'm not!" said Dougal, dodging a flying lolly stick. "Catch me! You can if you like."

But that idea did not seem to appeal to the toddlers' mothers at all. They wanted a rest from their responsibilities, and if necessary they were prepared to pay for it.

"How long does a ride take?" they asked.

"About fivish minutes," said Dougal crossly.

"So six would take half an hour?"

"I suppose," admitted Dougal, "but it would cost twelve pounds."

"Twelve pounds?" repeated the toddlers' mothers.

"Want to go wound and wound!" bawled the voices in the carriages, and then the one with the ice cream pushed it into the ear of the one with the candy floss, and all five began kicking the sides of the train.

Their mothers seemed to make up their

minds very suddenly.

"Six rides then," they said. "It's cheaper than the creche! We'll be back long before they are finished! Where does the money go? In that moose-nut bowl? Come on, let's run!"

"You're not leaving me with them?" demanded Dougal, appalled, but they were. They put their money in the moose-nut bowl and hurried away, calling, "Bye! Be good! Love you loads! What on earth is the matter with that moose?"

It was true that the furious and tethered Sir Lancelot was making a terrible noise, bellowing and roaring and kicking at the fence. The racket was almost as bad as the sound of the toddlers, wailing and slurping and demanding to go wound and wound.

"Crikey!" said Dougal, in disgust.

"WOUND AND WOUND!" commanded the toddlers at the tops of their voices.

"All right! Round and Round!" shouted Dougal, even louder. "Hold tight. You're going now!" and he reached for the green button to GO.

Then, with a terrible bellow Sir Lancelot reared high into the air, broke free from his rope, and charged.

Time seemed to go in slow motion.

"Wound and wound," murmured the largest toddler, and reached out and pressed the green button himself.

Up into the air rose Dougal, propelled there by the mighty impact of Sir Lancelot's charge.

"Clunk," went the little train, and started along the track.

Down floated Dougal, admiring the little white clouds overhead.

And then he landed.

Dougal could see stars, floating towards him like pinpoints of brightness and then zipping away again in lovely curves and swoops. He watched them happily. He had forgotten all about the Summer Fair and the Triple Terror Express. He had forgotten Kate and Madeline and Samuel and Simon. He had forgotten his own name.

After a time he began to realise that someone was washing his face. This was not so good because they were using a very warm rubbery flannel.

It was smelly too. It smelt of moose nuts.

"Geroff!" said Dougal.

It was as if he had broken a spell. Voices rained down on him from above, Samuel and Simon, Madeline and Samantha.

"Dougal, can you hear us?"

"Wake up, Dougal! Open your eyes!"

Dougal thought about doing that, dreamily, as if he was in a warm bed. He decided he couldn't be bothered.

"Move Sir Lancelot closer, Samuel,"ordered Madeline. "Perhaps he needs a bit more face washing!"

"I don't!"

Squinting against the brightness, Dougal peered up at them.

"He's still alive!" exclaimed Samantha, and then accidently very nearly knocked him out again by dropping a coconut that she had won on to his head.

"Ug," groaned Dougal, blinking and stretching. "Hello Samantha! You won't kill me with a coconut so you might as well stop trying. Hi, Simon! Samuel! Madeline! Why's everyone staring at me?"

"We thought you were dead," said Madeline. "We were looking from the top of the helter-skelter. We saw that you'd uncovered the little train, and we watched the toddlers getting on ..."

"We saw Sir Lancelot charge and shoot you up in the sky ..." continued Samuel.

"And we saw you come crashing down again," said Samantha. "And we thought you would be dead and we'd have to close the fair early and the whole day would be ruined ..."

"We rushed to help as fast as we could. No one else seemed to notice you at all. The toddlers never even glanced … Just reached out and pressed the button …"

"Where are those toddlers?" interrupted Simon suddenly.

They stared at Simon. And then they stared at Dougal. And then they rushed to inspect the Triple Terror Express.

It had finished its journey and was back out in the open again, perfectly silent and empty.

"Dougal!" said Madeline, accusingly.

"What?" asked Dougal, sitting up very carefully and feeling the back of his head to see if it actually was as flat as it felt. "Why are you all looking at me like that?"

"It's the little train!" said Samuel. "It smells of magic. Yesterday it smelt of mildew, and today it smells of magic …"

"And where are those toddlers?" demanded Madeline.

"I don't know," said Dougal, shrugging. "I'm

not a babysitter. Their mums must have come back and got them, I suppose."

"I think they're still inside," said Samantha unexpectedly.

"Inside where?"

"Inside the tunnel … Let me talk! Don't interrupt! I know it sounds stupid but a bit earlier this afternoon I saw Mrs Pooter climb on to the little train, all by herself …"

"What a cheek!" exclaimed Dougal. "Without paying!"

"She did pay. Well, she put something in Sir Lancelot's moose-nut bowl. I saw her bend down …"

Samantha darted for the bowl. Sure enough, there was a fifty pence piece below the two five pound notes and two pound coins put there by the toddlers' mothers.

"You see, she paid! And then she pressed the button and went off into the tunnel …"

"So what?"

"She didn't come out! And now those toddlers haven't come out either …"

Without meaning to, Sir Lancelot and Dougal glanced at each other. It was a guilty, unreliable look, and everybody saw it.

"Dougal McDougal!" said Madeline. "What have you and Sir Lancelot done to the little train?"

"Oiled it a bit," said Dougal sulkily.

"Oiled it?" asked Madeline. "I'm sure oiling isn't allowed! I'm sure it said that on the form the little man made me sign."

" 'Course it didn't," said Dougal, grumpily. "What a daft thing to say! Oiling's good for things. Me and Dad oil things all the time at home. You'd understand, Madeline, if you weren't just a girl."

"Don't call me just a girl!" said Madeline furiously. "I understand just as much as you,

112

Dougal McDougal! And I remember that there was a list of things that we weren't allowed to do and oiling was one of them. I think the form is still in the classroom. I'm going to look for it now! Come and help me, someone!"

She set off at a run back towards the school and Simon and Samuel went after her, which left Dougal and Samantha alone together.

Samantha said suspiciously, "I don't think just oiling it would make it start disappearing people!"

"Of course it's not disappearing people!" said Dougal. He had been sitting on the grass, holding on to his head which still felt terribly loose and wobbly, but now, by hanging on to Sir Lancelot's leg, he got shakily to his feet. "I'll prove it's not, Samantha Freebody!"

"Well, I'll prove it is, Dougal McDougal!" snapped Samantha, pushing past him. "Don't grab at me, you useless moose!"

A moment later she had pushed the green button, flounced neatly into the last carriage of the little train, and vanished.

There was a very tense silence. It lasted until the train reappeared and Samantha did not. Then Sir Lancelot kicked Dougal quite hard.

"Oh, leave me alone, Sir Lancelot!" wailed Dougal. "It was all your fault in the first place! Oh crikey! Oh no! Here come the toddlers' mums!"

"What have you done with them?" they demanded, standing over Dougal with their empty pushchairs.

"I haven't done anything with them," said Dougal indignantly. "You put them on the train! It wasn't my idea! Six rides, you said, while you had a bit of peace! Anyway, I thought you wanted to get rid of them!"

This tactless reply only seemed to infuriate

the two mothers more than ever.

"But where are they now?"

"In there," said Dougal, pointing, and added reluctantly, "We think they may have come off!"

"Come off?" they shouted. "What do you mean, come off?"

"Well, they haven't come out the other end, that's all ... No! Please don't try walking along the tracks. It's very oily ..."

It occurred to Dougal at that moment that the only thing to be done with the toddlers' mums was to put them onboard the little train too. Surely, he thought, it would be much better for them to be reunited with their offspring (wherever they were) than out here on the grass, worrying and shouting. So he said hopefully,

"Go on the train if you want to look for them ... it's quite comfy ... And only fifty pence each, not extra for adults!"

"Fifty pence?" they cried. "Fifty pence! We don't think so! And we'll take that, thank you very much!"

The twelve pounds that they had left in the moose-nut bowl was suddenly scooped out again, and then the toddlers' mothers were gone.

"You didn't try and stop them," said Dougal to Sir Lancelot.

Sir Lancelot shook his head.

"They'll be back in a minute, to yell at me some more. You wait and see!"

Sir Lancelot sighed, a great damp smelly moose sigh. And then he bent his knees and collapsed on to the grass beside Dougal. He looked a changed animal from the moose that had shown Dougal how to find the control panels early that morning. He looked noble and regretful, like a moose who planned from now on to be completely reliable, for ever and ever.

## CHAPTER SIX
### Going Inside

Dougal's fall had shaken him. His head was
very sore, and his brain was very confused.
Now he was alone, the summer fair, with the
magical ponies, the distant views from the
lighthouse and the sparkling splendour of the
dodgems, all felt like events in a dream. Even
though he himself had ridden on a pony that
swished its tail and tossed its head, and felt the
sea breeze at the top of the lighthouse and
driven a dodgem that skimmed away with its
own comet tail of coloured stars, Dougal could
not quite believe it was all really happening.

119

And the thing that he could not believe most was the the Triple Terror Spine Chilling Icy World Express was actually ...

"No, no, no, no, no, no," said Dougal, rocking his sore head.

"Dougal?" asked a voice, very close by. "What's the matter, Dougy?"

Kate was standing beside him, looking very puzzled.

"It's my train," said Dougal.

"Hasn't anyone come to ride on it?" asked Kate sympathetically.

"Not many. Good job too. It keeps disappearing people."

"How do you mean?"

"They get on. And they go into the tunnel. And then I think ... I think ... I think they might disappear."

"Gosh!" said Kate, beginning to laugh. "That's so useful, Dougy! I know a lot of people I'd like to put on your train!"

"It isn't funny!" cried Dougal in anguish.

"Dougal darling, don't be silly! I expect they crawl off halfway round."

"They don't."

"To trick you."

"It isn't like that," Dougal slumped down on the platform and his head sank lower and lower into his arms. Kate stared at him in dismay.

"They wouldn't mean to upset you. Just as a joke."

"You don't understand," said Dougal.

"I'll tell you what! I'll have a go! I promise not to disappear!"

Then, just as Samantha had done, Kate pressed the green button and climbed nimbly aboard.

Sir Lancelot's life as a noble, reliable moose began at that moment. He leapt on to the platform in front of the already moving train, placed his enormous head against the front of the engine and began to push. For a minute he and the Triple Terror Express were perfectly balanced, the train pushing forwards into the entrance of the tunnel, Sir Lancelot pushing back towards the open platform. But then Sir Lancelot slipped a little on a patch of oil. With horrible grinding sounds the Triple Terror Express began to move again, propelling Sir Lancelot slowly into the dark.

Kate and Dougal did not simply watch all this. The moment he realised what was happening, Dougal jumped up behind the train and grabbed hold of the last carriage and pulled. And as soon as Kate understood, she climbed out to help, too. But even together they could not stop the train. Bellowing, kicking, skidding on the oily tracks, Sir Lancelot gradually disappeared, first his tail

and then his middle, and finally his huge
flailing antlers.

"Don't let go!" panted Kate. "He'll be run
over if we do!"

But Sir Lancelot was not run over because
Madeline, Samuel and Simon arrived just as
the last carriage was disappearing into the
dark. With their strength to help, the train no
longer moved forward. Ice-cold air began to
pour from the tunnel, and with it a smell of
magic so strong it made Sir Lancelot's rescuers
giddy. Very slowly the little train reappeared,
backwards this time, and with it came Sir
Lancelot, first his antlers, then his middle and
finally his tail.

He was a changed Sir Lancelot. His coat
was so heavy with frost that he sparkled as if
he was covered in thick white glittering fur.
Icicles hung from his antlers. He steamed in
the sunshine so much that the whole corner of

the school field became lost in a chilly grey fog.

The struggle to rescue Sir Lancelot seemed to have unjammed something in the mechanism of the train, because the slot below the green button for GO suddenly began to churn out photographs. They fell in sticky strips to the floor, tangled together in bunches. Madeline and Dougal left Sir Lancelot to gather them up. Many of them were stuck face to face, or torn and twisted, but among them were plenty that were still clear.

They showed Dougal and Madeline the fate of the disappeared. There were the three big boys who had stolen a free ride, crouched in a snow fort, all their bounce gone. There were the toddlers, sucking icicles instead of lollipops and having ice-cold tantrums, flat on their backs. There were their mothers, longing

for peace, and there was the North Pole, a
dark glimmering pillar of twisted ice, rising
into the infinite Arctic night.

"Here's Samantha," said Dougal, faint with
thankfulness, and there was Samantha, with
frosted hair and startled eyes, under the blaze
of a sky full of green and purple rainbows.

"The Northern Lights?" wondered
Madeline, and Dougal remembered the

control that he had turned from "Back Up" to "Main".

There was also a photograph of what looked like a real live dragon.

"A real live dragon!" said Samuel, wonderingly. "Do you suppose it is?"

"Yes," said Dougal, "I know it's real live, because I set the dial on real live."

"I knew you hadn't just oiled it!" said Madeline. "Now tell us what you did!"

So Dougal confessed all his rash adjustments, starting with the * to reset, and ending with the dragons. And Madeline unfolded the delivery note that she had retrieved from the classroom and read aloud again:

"Contents not to be altered, adjusted, oiled or otherwise tampered with in any way. Otherwise Trouble-free Running Not Guaranteed at all!!!"

"Not Guaranteed at All!" repeated Madeline. "And the little men will be back to take everything away at 6 o'clock. Then what, Dougal McDougal, when they see what you've done!"

"It'll be the end of magic lessons with Miss Gilhoolie when she finds out," remarked Simon gloomily.

"It will be the end of all the passengers if you don't do something sooner than six o'clock!" said Kate severely. "They'll freeze to death, if the dragons don't get them!"

"It won't be the end of anything," said Dougal, crossly. "Not magic lessons, or the passengers or anything. I shall just adjust it back."

Even as he spoke, he was already beginning, on his hands and knees on the grass, tugging at the bolts that held the sections together.

"There's a control panel under each one,"

he explained over his shoulder. "Sir Lancelot showed me. I suppose he saw them setting it up. No wonder they asked if he was reliable ..."

Sir Lancelot, still billowing fog, hung his head in shame.

"I crawled underneath, very early this morning and made a few changes ... A lot of changes. I turned everything up to Max! It's no good waving that piece of paper at me, Madeline! I know I shouldn't have. I promise that as soon as I can get a section loose I'll go underneath and change everything back to how it was."

The trouble was, the sections would not come loose. Kate and Madeline pulled and prized, Dougal, Samuel and Simon levered and tugged and Sir Lancelot kicked. They managed to open the bolts but they could not get the sections apart. They succeeded in opening a small chink but that was all. The door at the entrance of the tunnel had been jammed slightly open when Sir Lancelot had been pulled out backwards. Because of this, all the time they were working, from inside the tunnel came waves of icy dark air, glimpses of eerie lights, and orange dragon fire.

"What I can't understand," said Madeline as she struggled with bolts, "is why no one has come out? Even if you did reset the controls, why didn't the train take them right through and out the other end?"

"Why didn't they just walk out?" wondered Samuel.

"You'd have to crawl," said Simon. "The tunnel's not that high."

"Crawl, then."

Dougal shook his head. He had wondered himself about the very same thing but he did not know the answer. All he could think was

that if he could only get to the control panels
he could reset them all to how they had been
that morning and everything would be all
right.

But he could not get to the control panels
because none of the sections would move an
inch.

"They're seized up," said Kate at last, "seized
up or rusted up or frozen up. We need oil."

That made Dougal think.

"There's plenty of oil inside," he said. "It's as
oiled as oiled in there. I dropped a whole tin
and the train ran over it. Perhaps, if someone
inside could lean against the North Pole and
really shove outwards, while everyone out
here pulled … Yes, that's the way to do it!
Lend me your jacket, Simon! Hold Sir
Lancelot, Madeline! Don't start crying, Kate!
It's no good any of you arguing, I'm going
inside … I may be some time …"

Dougal's heroic exit was slightly spoiled by Samuel saying perfectly calmly with no fuss at all, "I'll come too," and jumping into the carriage beside him. "It's an awful waste not to have a look at real live dragons when you get a chance," he added, taking off his glasses and polishing them so as not to see the dragons blurred. "Anyway, I can help push, can't I!"

" 'Course you can," said Dougal and stopped feeling sore headed and heroic and guilty and started feeling adventurous and cheerful instead. "Here's the tunnel ... hold tight ... WOW!"

It was not a tunnel, it was a landscape. A blue shadowy world of ice. On their left towered the North Pole, so tall that the top was hidden in the darkness above. On their right ice pillars and mountains rose all about them. Icy winds blew. Icy distances stretched into dim icy mists in every direction. Ahead the rails shone silver, a great curve of track along which the train was travelling at incredible speed. There was no one to be seen.

"I thought this tunnel must be bigger on the inside than the outside," said Samuel, in a very pleased voice.

"Crikey!" said Dougal, "Look at it! It must go on for miles! No wonder they didn't try and walk back! Hey, I adjusted this! Aren't you pleased I did, now? Isn't it freezing? Isn't it good? Admit it's a bargain for fifty pence!"

Samuel agreed that it was definitely a bargain for fifty pence, very good indeed, and extremely cold. The cold increased as the train ran faster and faster, speeding across the ice towards a thick black line that ran from North Pole to far horizon.

"Th ... th ... that must be the j ... j ... join to the next section," said Dougal through chattering teeth. "Where we v ... v ...

vanish … Ouch!"

There was an enormous jolt, the line flashed
black as the river of ice beneath the tracks of
the train, and everything went utterly dark.
Dougal reached out for Samuel and there was
nothing there. There was nothing anywhere.
He hugged himself and his vanished arms
passed through his non-existent body. It was
such an odd feeling that his voice was quite
quavery when he asked, "Are you still here,
Sam?"

"No," said Samuel happily. "Only the idea of
me is still here. I've vanished! You did brilliant
adjustments, Doug! I can't wait for the
dragons!"

He didn't have long to wait. They jolted
over the join to the next section, reappeared
as if they had never been gone, and gazed in
astonishment at a world turned gold. It was
the gleaming gold of sunlight reflected on ice,

but it was not sunlight. It was dragon fire. It came from the jaws of three huge green dragons.

"Cool!" said Samuel.

Dougal's brain skittered from one amazed thought to another as the train, now travelling quite slowly, grew closer and closer. They were the shape of crocodiles but the size of elephants! Several elephants, not just one! Were dinosaurs ever as big as this?

"They're the size of buses!" whispered Samuel.

The dragons the size of buses were acting very strangely, leaping and squirming and lashing their tails. A small figure moved among them. It stooped and rolled something across the ice and the dragons skidded away in pursuit.

"Samantha!" cried Dougal, and Samantha it was.

The train ground to a halt just as the three dragons came racing up to her.

"Sit!" cried Samantha. "Hello Samuel! Hello Dougal! It's all right, don't be frightened, they only want to play! This is brilliant! I always wanted to be an animal trainer! Good dragons! Clever dragons! Drop it then!"

The largest dragon dropped something small and black at Samantha's feet.

"It's that coconut I won earlier." said Samantha, touching it with her toe. "We'll just leave it to cool a minute. It's been so useful. They can balance it on their noses too, but it starts to smoke if they do it for long. I have to keep playing with them or else they go and bother the boys."

She nodded towards a group Dougal and Samuel had not yet noticed, the three big boys who had stolen their rides. They were huddled in a sulky group around the North Pole.

"They don't like it here," said Samantha. "They've been moaning and moaning! They say it's too cold (although they have got hoods) and there's no reception for their mobile phones, and there's nothing to do and it's boring. And they say the dragons aren't safe! Of course they're not safe! They're dragons! The toddlers' mums aren't happy, either, they're complaining to the secretary ... there, just behind you."

Mrs Pooter had been very efficient. She had built herself a cool white office entirely out of snow. It had a desk and a chair and a too-low sofa, just like her office in school. The toddlers' mums were sitting on the sofa making a list of complaints which the secretary was writing down as fast as she could.

"But where are the toddlers?" asked Dougal.

"Yes, that might be rather sad," said

Samantha, not sounding sad at all. "I'm afraid we've lost them. They fell down a little crack that opened up quite suddenly, just beside the North Pole. About twenty minutes ago ..."

"A crack?" asked Dougal jubilantly. "Hurray! That must be where we managed to start it moving from the outside. Come on, Samuel! All we've got to do is make it bigger."

"Watch out for the oil!" called Samantha. "There's a big patch of oil right next to it. That's how the toddlers fell. They skidded and went over the edge, one after another! Just like penguins jumping off a cliff on a natural history programme."

"But why didn't you all go down after them?" asked Dougal.

"It's very narrow. They only just fitted. Anyway, it didn't look the sort of place you'd want to go, on purpose."

"Well couldn't you just climb back on the

train and come out the other end?"

"The dragons won't let anyone on the train once they've got off," said Samantha. "You try it now and see!"

Dougal and Samuel obediently turned back towards the train. At once the three dragons stopped chasing the coconut and arranged themselves into a menacing green landscape, claw-edged, spine-peaked, smoke-wreathed. Their jaws became three enormous fire belching caverns pointing directly at Dougal and Samuel. Six yellow reptilian eyes seem to glare straight into their suddenly pounding hearts.

"Told you so," said Samantha.

Dougal and Samuel agreed that she had, and turned back towards the crack down which the toddlers had disappeared. As they got closer they saw that Samantha's description was correct. It really did not look the sort of place you'd want to go on purpose, a narrow gash in the ice that seemed to drop to bottomless black depths. The three big boys, who had been idly hacking chunks from the North Pole, looked closely at Dougal as he came towards them, and then muttered to each other under their hoods. Then the biggest of them stepped very near to Dougal and said, "You owe us an explanation, mate! And if you know what's good for you, you'll get us out of here. Them dragons of yours are out of control!"

"You owe me one pound fifty," replied Dougal with spirit. "But you are quite right. They are my dragons, and they are out of control. So if you know what's good for you, you'll pay right now and then come and help me and Samuel push! We"ve got to get that crack big enough to go down and make some adjustments."

The big boys pushed back their hoods and stared at Dougal.

"You're mad," they said and paid over their one pound fifty with no fuss at all. Mad people worried them even more than dragons and boredom. They agreed to help push too, leaning their backs against the North Pole and digging their feet into the ice. However, they refused to stand close to the crack.

"It was 'orrible watching them little kids go over," they told Samuel and Dougal. "One squeal and that was it! Look, you can see where their fingers scrabbled at the edge!

"They'll have landed on grass," said Dougal hopefully. "It's not as deep as it looks. It's just a little space where we managed to get the sections apart. Can you push again? It's definitely getting wider. I suppose Madeline and the others are pulling on the outside too."

One more push, and not only did the crack

141

get wider, but a wedge-shaped gap suddenly opened up at the base of the North Pole. They jumped back just in time to avoid tumbling into it. It looked like a long, narrow letterbox in the ice, an opening into a thousand metres of bottomless dark. Grey mists swirled up from the depths. Over head the Northern Lights flared purple and green. The big boys shuddered and stepped back.

"It's quite safe," said Dougal. "It comes out into the school playing field."

"Theoretically," said Samuel, thoughtfully.

"I think that's what they call an abyss," said Samantha, coming across to peer over. "Those poor toddlers. Be careful you don't land on their bodies. I bet you wish you'd brought a rope. Why did you say you want to go down there?"

"It's the only way to reach the control panels."

"You'd better get on with it then," said Samantha. "Poor you (even though this is all your fault). It looks absolutely horrible. What shall we do if you never come back? Are you going to jump or slide? Do you want us to do a countdown? Do you think that would help?"

"No, I don't think it would," said Dougal, who sat down, slid his legs over the crack, and let go.

It was a strange feeling, plunging from one world to another, from the burning colours of the Northern Lights to the darkness of the chasm, from ice to summer grass, from the hiss and roar of dragon fire to the sounds of

fairground music and cheerful voices.

Not that the first voice Dougal heard was very cheerful. It said, very tiredly, "Want to go wound and wound!"

"Oh!" exclaimed Dougal joyfully, trying to sit up and bumping his head on the bottom of the little wooden platform. "My baby! My baby! Kate! Madeline! Can you hear me? We've found the rest, Samantha and Mrs Pooter and everyone. Have you got all the toddlers there safe? All five?"

"Dougal!" called Madeline. "How brilliant! Yes, we've got all five. Very, very dirty. They fell down a crack …

"Cwack!" corrected a very grumpy voice.

"… And dug a tunnel. They crawled out a few minutes ago …"

"Cwarled," said the voice.

"We've fed them and watered them, well hot-dogged and coca-cola-ed them, and Sir

Lancelot washed their faces but they didn't like it much. Dougal, you must hurry up! The lorries will be here soon. Everyone's packing away!"

"I'm hurrying up," said Dougal, "I've started already."

Flat on his back, he shuffled around the sections of the little train, searching for the luminous controls.

The first one he found was the only one he had not seen before. It was on the sixth section.

I never thought of there being one there! thought Dougal.

It was the most important of all.

Only to be Used With Maximum Power Settings! (it read)
Journey Specification
Single/Return

It was set on Single.

No wonder no one ever came back! thought
Dougal, and flipped it to Return.

From that point he worked backwards,
changing Dragons from "Live" to "Illustrated",
Northern Lights from "Main" to "Back Up",
Darkness from "Utter and Complete" to
"Simulated" and Icy Cavern from "Max" to
"Min". And last of all he reached the one that
read:

"NO UNAUTHORISED ACCESS!

To Reset Controls Press *

It was with the most enormous feeling of relief
Dougal once again pressed *.

And all that he needed to do after that was to
slightly enlarge the tunnel that the toddlers
had made and crawl out on to the grass.

"Shush!" whispered Kate, as he finally appeared. "Your toddlers have just fallen asleep with Sir Lancelot!"

To Madeline, Kate and Simon it seemed hardly any time between the moment Dougal emerged from the toddlers' tunnel to the arrival of the little train.

To the passengers of the Triple Terror Express it took much longer.

"Well, everything is bigger in there," said Samuel, "Distances and time and cracks in the ice ... It was horrible watching you go down that hole, Dougal, and you were so long we thought you had stuck. Samantha lowered me as far as she could by my ankles but I couldn't see much."

"It was a long way down," agreed Dougal, remembering the immense icy slopes down which he had hurled between worlds. "When did you notice I'd reset the controls?"

"When it all began changing," said Samantha. "The dragons were the first thing. They suddenly started rounding people up, just like sheepdogs. And as soon as they had everyone together in a bunch they chased them on to the train.

"Ah," said Dougal, and remembered how he had switched the Journey Specification from Single to Return.

"After that things happened quite quickly," continued Samuel. "The Northern Lights faded and went out and the train began to move."

"An awful smell of mildew seemed to come from all around," said Samantha.

"Instead of magic," explained Samuel regretfully.

"I threw the coconut one last time for the dragons ... they were lovely dragons ... and they ran off into the distance ..."

"Then suddenly there wasn't any distance," said Samuel. "Just the end of the tunnel, and here we are."

The little train had been packed when it came out. Mrs Pooter with the toddlers' mums at the front, the big boys and Samuel in the carriages behind, and last of all Samantha, waving rather tearfully to her vanished dragons. And just as distances and times that had seemed enormous in the icy world shrank in real life, so did the problems.

The mothers of Dougal's toddlers, after an amazed but silent reunion with their families, scooped them up as carefully as if they were handling unexploded bombs, lowered them into their pushchairs and silently tiptoed away.

The school secretary put her list of complaints carefully aside for the recycling box, and said, "These things always give me such a head! How much have you made, dears? Two pounds? Really! Jolly good!" And then she left as well.

The three big boys, who had taken a liking to Dougal, kindly invited him to go shoplifting with them the following morning. Dougal said thanks very much, but he thought he would be too tired.

Samantha said, "It's terribly, terribly sad about my dragons … OOOHHHH!"

After that she went home very quickly, carrying the moose-nut bag.

"What we ought to do," said Samuel, when there was just himself and Simon and Kate and Dougal and Madeline left gathered around the little train, "is to have one last go to make sure it is truly safe."

"I'd rather have one last go on the dodgems," said Dougal, and that started everyone off. Kate and Madeline rushed to the carousel, and Simon to the lighthouse.

So only Samuel tried out the Triple Terror
Spine Chilling Icy World Express for the very
last time.

And was it back to totally boring?" asked
Dougal, as they walked home together, after
that long afternoon.

"Totally."

"Plastic icicles?"

"Yes, and that black dangly curtain."

"Those rubbish light bulbs for the Northern
Lights?"

"Yes. Just the same."

"Completely unscary cartoon dragons
drawn on the walls?"

"So completely unscary I didn't even notice
them," said Samuel, reassuringly.

## CHAPTER SEVEN
### What Happened In The End

"Back on Monday!" Miss Gilhoolie had
promised, and back on Monday she was,
deliciously dressed in black and silver lace
over sea-green silk. Her orange hair was piled
high up on her head to show off new diamond
earrings and her shoes (which were the exact
green of her dress) had very high silver heels.

"It is lovely to see you again," she told Class
4b, and they replied very admiringly that it
was lovely to see her too.

"You don't look a bit ill anymore," observed

Simon happily.

"I am not a bit ill anymore," replied Miss Gilhoolie complacently, filling in the register at the speed of light. "I have made a complete recovery. I always do. No Samantha with us today? Can anyone tell me whether she is Poorly or Just Very, Very Late?"

"She may be poorly," said Charlotte. "Emma and I went round to her house on Saturday to see if she wanted to play. But she wouldn't. Her mum said she had locked herself in her bedroom with some bananas and cat food and buckets of water, so we thought she could not be well."

"Hmmmm," said Miss Gilhoolie. "Perhaps. Well. Tell me about the school summer fair! I trust you won the Special Class Prize?"

Class 4b shook their heads. The amounts raised at the summer fair had already been counted. Class 4a were telling anyone who would listen that they had taken the lead by an incredible, triumphant, seven hundred pounds.

"Oh really!" said Miss Gilhoolie. "that is rather disappointing. Still, you must have come second, anyway?"

Everyone turned to look at Madeline, who had taken charge of the money and kept the accounts. She passed the account sheet to Miss Gilhoolie, together with a very small jam jar.

"Goodness," said Miss Gilhoolie, peering into the jam jar and then reading the list. "How on earth did you manage to do so badly? And how can you possibly account for Moose Shampoo as a necessary expense?"

"I suppose it does seem odd," murmured Madeline.

The moose shampoo had been bought on

Saturday morning. Madeline and Dougal had gone to check up on Sir Lancelot and they had been quite shocked at the state he was in. The day before, in all the hurry and crowds of the summer fair he had not seemed so bad. But now the fair was gone, every last trace packed up and magicked away, and Sir Lancelot stood alone in the middle of the green grass playing field.

And he looked awful.

"Not a bit reliable," said Madeline, and Dougal agreed. Sir Lancelot had always been a scruffy animal. He was always muddy in winter, and dusty in summer. No amount of brushing ever quite got rid of it, nor of the moose-nut dribble that stained his front green. But now, in addition to his usual grubbiness, he was dappled from antlers to hoofs in bike oil, and, on top of that, he was smeared all over with a dreadful stickiness that had wiped off the toddlers.

Even more noticeable than those things, however, was the enormous smell of magic that surrounded him like smog. No mixture of healthy hedgehogs, French perfume, old boots, pine-scented snow and sea winds ever smelt as strong as Sir Lancelot did the morning after the school summer fair.

"If Miss Gilhoolie gets a sniff of that on Monday, she will know straight away that something went wrong," Dougal said. "However did he get so bad?"

"Getting stuck in that tunnel must have done it," said Madeline. "He was absolutely covered in magic ice when he came out. I suppose it defrosted and dried on him. Poor old Lancelot! We will have to wash him."

"Wash him?"

"Yes."

"What with?"

"Moose shampoo, of course," said Madeline.
It took thirty-six bottles of moose shampoo
to make Sir Lancelot smell like anything
approaching a reliable moose. Even then the
results were not perfect.

"How," enquired Miss Gilhoolie on Monday morning, "did Sir Lancelot manage to get unclean enough to require scrubbing with thirty-six bottles of moose shampoo (price £19.99 a bottle)? How could any moose possibly get so dirty, simply by standing in a perfectly clean field?"

Once again everyone turned to poor Madeline. Luckily, however, she was saved from trying to answer this very difficult question by the sudden arrival of Samantha, who came racing in to the classroom wearing oven gloves and looking very hot.

"Good morning, Miss Gilhoolie," she panted and dropped the biscuit tin she was carrying with a sigh of relief.

"Good morning, Samantha! You are very late! Is that your lunch in that tin, or something else?"

"Something else," said Samantha, poking it

under her desk with her foot, and blushing very red. "I'm sorry I'm late Miss Gilhoolie, and my mum said I've got to tell you … got to tell you … got to tell you …"

"Yes, Samantha?"

"No more pets to be brought home from school!"

"But have you taken any pets home from school?" asked Miss Gilhoolie, very surprised.

"No, Miss Gilhoolie, but still she said to tell you."

"Very odd," said Miss Gilhoolie. "Goodness, there is a strange smell in this room! Samantha, is that tin …"

Again, Miss Gilhoolie was interrupted in the middle of an awkward question, this time by Mrs Pooter. She held an enormous green and yellow envelope addressed in very curly, very twirly, very black writing.

"Special delivery, Miss Gilhoolie," she

panted, "So I brought it along straight away."

"Thank you Mrs Pooter," said Miss Gilhoolie. "Mrs Pooter, can you smell scorching in here?"

"I can't smell anything with my hay fever," said Mrs Pooter. "It affects my eyes too, otherwise I would say that although I cannot smell scorching I do perceive a Slight Blue Haze. I must get on, dear! Goodbye children! They behaved beautifully last week while you were away, Miss Gilhoolie!"

"Oh good," said Miss Gilhoolie, but Dougal and Madeline thought she looked very unconvinced, and Samantha, secretly fanning her biscuit tin, went redder than ever.

Then Miss Gilhoolie opened the green and yellow envelope and discovered a brief but furious note from the owners of the fair saying Three Items had Been Discovered Missing.

"Which if not returned immediately will

bring about Unfortunate but Drastic Consequences," read Miss Gilhoolie aloud. "Who can explain this, please?"

No one could. Class 4b looked at each other, completely and honestly puzzled.

All except Samantha, who said in a very small voice, "I'm afraid I've got them under my desk."

And then she pulled on her oven gloves once again, and opened the biscuit tin to reveal three minute but perfect green dragons, about as big as hamsters but much, much hotter.

When the dragons saw Miss Gilhoolie they ran round and round the tin in excitement and became very smoky and scorchy indeed.

"Simon and Samuel, open some windows, for goodness sake!" ordered Miss Gilhoolie, as the slight blue haze became suddenly much thicker. "Samantha, if you keep trying to stroke them they will never cool down! It only makes them more excited. And would you kindly explain how you happen to have them in the first place?"

"They fell down the crack," said Samantha. "They were running after the coconut one last time. I trained them, you see, to fetch coconuts. On the Triple Terror Express after Dougal had done his adjustments. They came out much smaller than they were on the inside (Samuel says everything from the Triple Terror Express is much bigger on the inside than the outside) so I scooped them up and took them home in Sir Lancelot's moose-nut bag. But my mum wasn't pleased. That's why she said to tell you no more pets. It has been a very difficult weekend."

Then, while the dragons cooled on the windowsill, the whole story of the school summer fair was dragged from Class 4b. Very soon there was nothing Miss Gilhoolie did not know. Every detail, from the arrival of the lorries to Dougal's heroic plunge into the icy chasm to correct his adjustments was revealed to her.

"It was not entirely your faults," said Miss Gilhoolie at last. "You should never have had that train. It was ordered by mistake. I would never have sent you anything so dangerous. But all the same, didn't you know that fair was magic? Didn't it look magic? Didn't it act magic? Didn't it smell magic? Haven't I taught you not to meddle with anything that smells of magic?"

"Yes," said everyone, and Dougal stood up and said very bravely, "It wasn't them, Miss Gilhoolie. It was me. It was all my fault."

"Oh well," said Miss Gilhoolie, smiling a little. "I suppose if you don't learn one way, you'll learn another."

"I've learnt now," said Dougal.

"You've lost the Special Class Prize though," said Miss Gilhoolie. "Class 4a will get it. Wasting all that money on moose shampoo! And I am afraid what is left in the jam jar will have to go on a special courier to take back the dragons."

"What was the prize?" wondered Simon, aloud.

"It is a trip to a theme park," Miss Gilhoolie told them. All rides free! I'm glad you find that funny, Dougal McDougal!"

"It would never have been as good as your fair," said Dougal.

"Wasn't it good?" asked Miss Gilhoolie, her eyes beginning to sparkle as brightly as her diamonds. "I remember when I first saw it when I was a little girl! The carousel and the dodgems and that wonderful helter-skelter! We saw a treasure island from the top!"

"We saw whales," Simon told her. "And icebergs and seals and dophins all jumping!"

"And the Triple Terror Express!" continued Miss Gilhoolie. "Oh yes, we all make mistakes, I've been there too! The icy cavern, and the Northern Lights! But you can't keep dragons as pets, no matter how small they become on the outside. They don't survive bedrooms, I'm afraid, and even if they did, I don't think the bedrooms would survive the dragons."

Miss Gilhoolie looked so fondly at the dragons as she spoke that Class 4b could not help wondering if one day, long ago, she had had first-hand experience of trying to keep dragons as pets in a bedroom.

"Don't look so upset, Samantha!" she said when the courier arrived to take them away. "They won't forget you, and I am sure you will see them again one day."

Samantha was allowed to put on her oven gloves one last time, and pack them carefully away in a special green and yellow fireproof box.

Everyone felt rather depressed when the dragons had gone, and they gazed around at the plain sunny ordinary world as if something was missing.

All except Dougal McDougal, who said, "Miss Gilhoolie?"

"Mmm?" asked Miss Gilhoolie, who also looked rather forlorn.

"There's still Sir Lancelot. We could go out and sniff him."

"Sniff the moose?"

"Just to remind us."

"Just to remind you?"

"Of the smell of magic. He still smells quite strong, when you get up close. Thirty-six bottles wasn't really enough."

"I'm very pleased to hear it."

"So could we go now? Straight away, do you think?"

"I don't see why not," said Miss Gilhoolie.

Mrs Pooter looked out of her window at Class 4b as they ran outside and she thought, Dear children! Dear Miss Gilhoolie! How very happy they seem to have her back again!

**More Pudding Bag School adventures:**

97S 0 340 97017 1

HILARY McKAY

PUDDING
BAG
SCHOOL

Cold Enough for Snow

978 0 340 97018 8

# Cold Enough for Snow

## CHAPTER ONE

On the day that the weather finally became cold enough for snow, Class 4b, Pudding Bag School, were given dinner ladies' detention. Nobody escaped. Dinner that day had been Mock Cod Pie and Class 4b had refused to eat it.

"And it was delicious beautiful home cooking," said Mrs Muldoon, the chief dinner lady. "The finest fish!"

"In a light cheese sauce," chimed in Miss Spigot, the second dinner lady. "With a mashed potato top."

"And padding!"

That was Amelia Pilchard, the third and last dinner lady. Mrs Muldoon was large and purple and Miss Spigot was bony and blue, but

Amelia Pilchard blended into the landscape like fog. Miss Pilchard was an padding expert. That meant she was very good indeed at mixing extra and unexpected ingredients into recipes, in order to make them go further.

"Perhaps it was the padding that caused the problems," suggested Miss Gilhoolie, Class 4b's teacher when she heard about her class's refusal to eat.

"It was wonderful padding," said Mrs Muldoon. "You could never have told it wasn't natural! The problem was caused by that redheaded Dougal McDougal! He started them all off, hiccuping and choking and making remarks!"

This sounded more than likely to Miss Gilhoolie. She knew Dougal McDougal very well indeed. He was very often the beginning of trouble. So she sighed but said to Mrs Muldoon, "In that case I suppose detention it must be. Poor dears! I will let their families know you are keeping them at school."

That was how Class 4b came to be alone in Pudding Bag School with nobody with them but the three dinner ladies. That was where they were when the first snowflake fell.

Nobody noticed it. It vanished before it touched the ground.

But it was the first of millions.

Dinner ladies' detention took place in the dining hall, a high-windowed, echoing and very chilly place. Class 4b were given paper and pencils and the menu board to copy out twenty times each as punishment, and the dinner ladies left them to huddle in the warmth of the cleaner's cupboard.

Simon Percy, who kept a diary, copied down the menu from the menu board as Madeline Brown read it out.

## MOCK COD PIE / MILD MIXED ROOT CURRY

## RUSSIAN TRIFLE / JELLY SURPRISE

*All made from the finest ingredients*

"All made from the *same* ingredients!" commented Dougal McDougal. "The only difference between the trifle and the pie was that one had bits of beetroot and the other had bits of fish. And the jelly had beetroot in as well."

"The trifle," remarked Simon, "had mashed potato on it! Lend me a line-writer somebody!"

Line-writers had been invented by Madeline Brown, the school brain, and manufactured by Mr Bedwig, ex-caretaker. You slid your paper into a wooden frame and a simple mechanism of cogs and levers allowed ten pencils to write at once. Simon was handed half a dozen line writers by people who had already completed their twenty of the menu board.

"I do miss Mr Bedwig," he remarked, as he set to work, and there was a murmur of agreement from all around. Mr Bedwig had worked at Pudding Bag School the term before and no caretaker could have been more useful. He had actually helped Class 4b build a rocket that had successfully blasted their frightful headmaster into space. The rocket had been designed by Madeline, but it had been Mr Bedwig who collected most of the parts and carried out the actual welding. Also, he had brought home Simon Percy's long-lost parents, redecorated the entire school, installed solar panels on the roof and an escape tunnel in the basement, banished chewing gum for ever, and adopted a cat.

Then, when everyone was just settling

down to live happily ever after, he had announced that he was needed elsewhere, and vanished.

"At least he left the cat," said Madeline. The cat, Bagdemagus, was curled up on her lap. He was the warmest thing in the school. "I wonder …"

Right in the middle of Madeline's wonder the dining-hall door was pushed open and Kate McDougal, Dougal's eighteen-year-old sister, blew into the room. Dougal had seven older sisters. Kate was his favourite. She was the youngest and prettiest and kindest, and by far the most excitable. Right now she was glowing with cold and excitement.

"What are you all doing, still at school?" she demanded. "Darling Dougal, I brought your wellies! Hadn't you better come home straight away? I've never seen such snow!"